TERRY DEARY

Stone Age Tales

The Great Cave

Illustrated by
Tambe

BLOOMSBURY EDUCATION
AN IMPRINT OF BLOOMSBURY

LONDON OXFORD NEW YORK NEW DELHI SYDNEY

Stone Age Tales
The Great Cave

BLOOMSBURY EDUCATION
Bloomsbury Publishing Plc
50 Bedford Square, London, WC1B 3DP, UK

BLOOMSBURY, BLOOMSBURY EDUCATION and
the Diana logo are trademarks of Bloomsbury Publishing Plc

First published in Great Britain in 2018 by Bloomsbury Publishing Plc

A catalogue record for this book is available from the British Library

ISBN: PB: 978 1 4729 5031 4; ePub: 978 1 4729 5032 1; ePDF: 978 1 4729 5030 7

2 4 6 8 10 9 7 5 3 1

Text design by Amy Cooper Design

Printed and bound in the UK by CPI Group (UK) Ltd, Croydon CR0 4YY

All papers used by Bloomsbury Publishing Plc are natural, recyclable products from
wood grown in well managed forests. The manufacturing processes conform to the
environmental regulations of the country of origin

To find out more about our authors and books visit www.bloomsbury.com
and sign up for our newsletters

Contents

1

Willow

17,300 years ago; Lascaux in France

They called the weak boy Willow. The strong boys were given strong names: Oak and Rock, Bull and Bone. But willow trees bent in the wind and drooped by the river. Willow limped after the hunters with his twisted leg but was never fast enough to be there at the kill.

The chief of the tribe was Flint, when Willow was young. Flint's hair was grey as the stone in the caves where they made their home. 'They say he's thirty-five winters old,' Willow's mother whispered to him one morning. 'They say he'll soon be dead.'

Willow nodded. 'Who'll be chief then?' he asked.

The woman shook her ragged head of hair as she fastened a cloak of rabbit skins round Willow's neck. 'The best hunter, I suppose.'

A fire flickered on the floor of the cave. Bones from last night's meal lay near it. Suddenly, two great hounds bounded into their hut and snapped at the leg-bone of a deer.

A man hurried in after them. 'Don't let the dogs eat, Rainbow,' he grumbled at Willow's mother. 'I want them hungry for the hunt.'

The man snatched at the bone but the dog, swift and grey as a rain-cloud, fled through the door and into the daylight outside.

'Sorry, Flint,' Rainbow moaned. 'I should have buried them.'

The man's anger slipped away and he sighed. 'Never mind,' he said with a small smile. 'Perhaps we'll make another kill today and we'll all eat well come darkness. Dogs and men.'

Willow picked up a wooden spear with a stone tip that he'd rubbed as sharp as one of Rainbow's bone-needles. 'I'm ready,' he said, eager and bright-eyed.

Flint lowered himself onto the warm deer skins on the floor. He was slow and stiff and Willow thought he heard the old man's bones creak.

'You could stay at home with the women,' he said. 'There are skins in the main cave. They need to be sewn together to make warm clothes for winter. You could help.'

Willow's mouth fell open. He swallowed tears. 'I'm a man... nearly,' he said. 'I want to hunt. Don't make me stay with the women.'

Flint nodded at Willow's twisted leg. 'You can't keep up, boy. You've tried. You know you can't.'

Willow's face burned red. 'I can carry the meat back to the caves,' he argued. 'Don't make me stay behind.'

Flint shrugged. 'I'm not much faster myself,' he sighed. 'There was a time when I could run alongside a horse and bring it down. No one else in the tribe could do that.'

'I wish I'd seen that,' Rainbow said with a sigh. 'But now you make plans. You are wise. You find the tracks and tell the hunters where to hide. Now you let the others do the running, Flint.'

The old man nodded and struggled to his feet. Willow stretched out a hand to help him. 'Come along, boy,' Flint said. 'We'll limp along at the back together, eh?'

Willow grinned. 'A deer or a horse or a bull will die today,' he said.

The old man and the boy shuffled up the slope towards the mouth of the cave. One of them would not walk back.

2

Bull

The women were scraping the flesh off skins and sewing them into clothes with sharp, bone needles. The young hunters were excited; pushing and wrestling and having mock fights to keep warm.

The boy called Bull was just one winter older than Willow, but had grown much larger. He was shouting to the other young men to keep quiet and sit on the ground.

When they had settled he spoke in a voice as deep as any man's. 'Today we hunt in the valley of the lilies. There are bison grazing there.'

'They will run away as soon as they see us,' old Flint said. 'We can't run fast as a bison.'

Bull threw back his head and laughed. 'You can't run as fast as a worm, old man,' he said with a sneer. 'But we aren't all as slow as you.'

Flint pulled a stone knife from his belt and pointed it at the boy. 'I am your chief. I will send you away from the tribe and let you starve in the forests.'

Bull's heavy face turned red with anger. He half-raised the hunting spear he was carrying. Everyone in the tribe fell silent. They waited.

'Maybe you won't be chief much longer. Maybe the spirit in the sky will take you soon,' Bull said.

The chief spoke quietly. 'Maybe she will. But, until that day, you *will* obey me.' He looked around the hunters. 'Now who is going to tell me the plan for today?'

'We were going to run down the valley and kill a bison,' a young man called River said. 'Maybe one of the old bison will be too stiff to run so fast.'

'If it's as old as me then it will be too tough to eat,' the chief said and gave a harsh laugh. The hunters smiled. All except Bull.

Willow stepped forward. 'The valley of the lilies is narrow with steep sides,' he said. 'If some of us make a noise with sticks and drums the bison will run. If the rest of us are at the far end of the valley then the bison will run straight onto our spears.'

'It might work,' Owl said.

Bull stepped forward. 'I will lead the hunters at the far end of the valley. I will make the kill,' he said in his booming voice. He pointed to ten hunters to go with him.

'We'll go to the far end of the valley now. When we are ready then River will give the howl of a wolf. That will be the signal for you to start your beating and driving the herd.'

Bull led ten others off at a run. They would circle around the hill and lay the trap.

Willow looked across to his mother, Rainbow. She nodded at him. 'You are clever, lad. Just like your mother.'

Flint placed an arm round the boy's shoulder. 'One day he will make a fine chief of the tribe... when I have gone to the spirit in the sky.' He looked at the women and girls who remained in the camp. 'Remember that. When I am gone, then Willow should be your chief.'

No one argued. Flint shuffled down the dusty track and Willow went to pick up one of the drums. Some of the tribe would not want him as chief, he knew. There would be one who would fight him for it. And he knew he would lose.

Willow sighed and limped off after Flint.

3
Bison

Willow and Flint walked through the dying ferns and grass. The spirit of winter was marching across the land. There would be four moons of hunger for the tribe. They held deer-skin drums in their hands and waited for the howl from River that would tell them the hunters were ready at the far end of the narrow valley.

A family of three bison were chewing on a patch of grass and drinking from the small stream. Willow shivered. 'Are you scared, boy?' Flint asked. He crouched down and spoke quietly so the bison wouldn't hear them.

'No, I'm not scared. Some evil spirit just made me shiver. Something bad will happen today,' Willow replied.

The old chief nodded. 'Your father died two summers ago. We grew up together.'

Willow nodded.

'Your father, Moss, was our painter. He went into a great, secret cavern and painted what we see when we hunt: the bison, the horses, the deer and the hunters. It kept the good spirits happy.'

'It brought us luck,' Willow said quietly.

'Since we've had no painter, our luck has run away from us. There are more evil spirits in the air – the ones you felt just now. The hunting was poor last summer. The hunters are hungry and getting angry. That's why a young, hot-blooded boy like Bull can stir up so much trouble for me,' Flint explained.

'But we will make a kill today,' Willow said, looking at the peaceful, grazing animals.

Flint gave a tired sigh. 'That is a cow with twin calves,' he said, soft as the stirring grass. 'A bull can charge if it's angry but he usually likes to run away. A bull is stupid.'

Willow gave a small smile when he thought of the other Bull – the young hunter.

Flint went on, 'A cow with calves wants to protect them. She is more dangerous than a starving bear.'

The cow seemed peaceful enough but Willow frowned. 'So will our hunters be in danger? Was my plan foolish?'

The chief blew out his creased, grey cheeks. 'So long as they stay hidden till the last moment,' he whispered. 'She will be at full speed, trying to watch her little ones. The dogs will be trying to grab her legs. She won't even see the hunters till the first spears strike her.'

'Will our friends stay hidden, the way you say?' the boy asked. 'I didn't tell them that.'

'That was my job,' Flint said. 'Let's hope our friends do what's right.'

At that moment the howl of a wolf echoed up the valley. 'That's River's signal,' the chief said. He rose stiffly to his feet.

The bison cow looked round in fear and

gave a snort to call her calves to her side. She looked down the valley and heard the cry a wolf. She looked up the valley and saw two humans beating drums.

Her small brain said it would be easier to use her sharp horns on a wolf, rather than two humans.

The bison began to trot down the valley between steep cliff walls, away from Willow and Flint. But before she'd gone a hundred paces another human stepped into the path, screaming and shaking a spear.

'It's Bull,' Willow groaned. 'He came out too soon. She'll kill him.'

But the cow saw Bull's spear and ten other hunters stumbling up the path to help him. There were too many for her to fight.

She turned and pushed her calves back the way they had come. She headed back towards an easier target... an old man with a stone knife and a limping boy with a spear. The cow put her head down so the spikes of her huge, curving horns pointed at them.

She began to charge.

4
Flint

Willow had faced charging animals before but he had always stood as one of a line of hunters. Their spears made a wall of spikes like bristles on a wild boar's snout. This time he stood alone except for his chief, who was armed only with a stone knife.

Willow dropped his drum and held the spear in front of him with the tip pointing upwards. He saw Bull and the hunters freeze and watch and wait for him to be crushed.

The ground trembled a little under the hooves of the cow, heavy as a boulder. Her fierce eyes were fixed on him. She was ten paces away when those eyes turned away.

Flint had stepped up to Willow's right shoulder and waved his knife at the beast.

She turned her massive head and headed towards the chief instead. In a few heartbeats she was onto them.

As her head struck the old man, Willow thrust the spear at it. The beast stumbled and fell and the spear was snatched out of Willow's hand.

Old Flint lay on the ground, bleeding and broken. The calves raced on into the woods and safety as the hunters ran up the valley towards their dying chief.

Bull was first to reach the place where Flint lay moaning softly. He stuck his spear into the cow and then raised the point above his head.

'I killed it,' he cried. 'Hurry,' he called to the running hunters. 'We need to get back to the village quickly.'

'Be careful,' Willow cried. 'He's badly hurt.'

'Oh, never mind old Flint,' the boy sneered. 'He's finished. We'll have a new chief before darkness falls tonight. We need to get the cow back and start butchering it. We'll feast for a week on this and smoke some flesh to get us through the winter.'

The hunters helped Bull drag the dead animal back up the valley to the village. Flint's face was white with pain. 'You saved me,' Willow said.

'I am ready to join the spirits,' the old man said. 'But you must be the next chief of the tribe. They need someone with your cleverness.'

'Let me help you back to the camp. My mother is good at curing broken bones. She healed my leg when the boulder crushed it years ago.'

Flint's brown eyes stared up towards the high clouds in the pale sky. The sun slipped out from behind one and lit up the valley, but Flint said, 'It's growing dark, boy. Get back to the village. Tell them I have gone to join all our fathers. Tell them you must be the chief.'

'I can't leave you here for the wolves,' Willow cried.

But Flint didn't reply.

Willow turned and limped back to where the cheering, excited tribe members were taking their flint knives to the cow. Every part of the kill would be used – the flesh, the sinews, the bones and the skin.

Everyone from the youngest child to the oldest man and woman found a job to do – everyone except Bull, who strutted around and laughed. 'My kill! Remember I get the first and finest flesh when it's roasted.'

Willow spoke quietly so only Bull could hear. 'Flint is dead.'

Bull shrugged. 'He had his time.'

'You killed him,' Willow said. 'You should have waited. The cow charged us because you didn't do what Flint told you to do.'

Bull's eyes went narrow. 'Flint died because he was too slow and old to get out of the way.'

'He said he wanted me to be the next chief.'

Bull leaned forward and poked the boy with the shaft of his spear. 'You are wrong, weak, little Willow. I heard him say he wanted *me* to be chief. The other hunters heard him.'

'They can't have done,' Willow said softly.

Bull gave another shrug and spoke just

as quietly. 'They will say they did if I tell them to. And you, Willow, will join Flint and the spirits if you argue.'

Willow looked at the spear pointed at his heart. 'If you say so, Bull.'

5

Cavern

Fat dripped onto the ashes of the fire where the meat hung over it. The ashes sizzled and flared, and then died to a red glow. The fire kept the wolves in the shadows away.

Bull stepped forward into the light and spoke in his booming voice. 'We need a new chief. You have all feasted on the beast I killed. I should be your chief.'

'You're young,' Owl said and a few of the tribe nodded and muttered to one another. 'Young.'

'I am young but I am the best hunter. The best leader.'

'Maybe you should fight to be leader, the way the stags do,' River argued.

For a moment Bull's eyes flickered in fear. He gave a small laugh. 'No, River. You see, good old Flint wanted *me* to be leader.'

'He told me last week that Willow would make a good leader when he grows a little older,' Owl said.

'Ah, that was before Willow got him hurt. It was Willow's mad plan to send all the hunters away down the valley and then face the bison alone. It was never going to work. Flint knew that. As he lay dying he saw that. He told me I should take his place as chief.'

River said, 'No one else heard him say that.'

Bull gave a smile. 'Willow heard him, didn't you, Willow? You heard Flint speak

the name of the next chief before he died, didn't you?'

'Yes, I heard him name the new chief, but...'

'See?' Bull cried. 'Old Flint named the chief before he went to join the spirits of our fathers. All those who want me for your leader say aye.'

The tribe well fed and sleepy now. 'Aye,' they murmured. 'Aye.'

Bull threw his spear into the ground and clapped his hands. 'You chose well,' he laughed. 'And my first act, as your new chief, is to rid this tribe of the weak. The feeble ones who eat but don't hunt to earn their food. Weak boys like Willow with his crushed leg.'

Willow's mother, Rainbow, struggled to her feet. 'He only has a crushed leg because *you* rolled a boulder onto it three summers ago.'

Bull ignored her and pointed at Willow. 'I won't kill you. Not yet. But if you are still here when the sun rises tomorrow then I shall. Get out.'

Willow turned and left the circle of red light. Foxes barked in the wood, wolves howled and somewhere a bear growled. Without his spear he would not last the night.

Suddenly he felt Rainbow's warm arm around him. 'Come with me, son,' she said.

The woman took a piece of animal skin and wrapped some berries and nuts in it along with a piece of the fresh, warm meat. She gathered another leather bag from the corner of her cave and pushed it into Willow's hands. Then she picked up a small lamp that was carved from stone,

gathered some of the animal fat from the fireside and lit the lamp.

'Where are we going?' Willow asked.

'To safety... to where you belong,' his mother told him.

Creatures rustled in the ferns as they walked by the edge of the forest and came to a low hill. Rainbow pulled away some branches that were piled in front of a cave and led the way.

The floor of the cave sloped down and, in the warm, dry air, there was not a sound. Rainbow raised the lamp towards the roof of the cave and Willow gasped at the sights he saw. 'What is this place?' he whispered.

'It's the cavern of the spirits,' his mother replied.

Willow shivered.

6

Paint

The oil lamp flickered with a smoky yellow light. It lit the walls and roof of the long cave. The walls were covered with paintings. There were horses, cows, bison and deer, as well as hunters. The red, yellow and black shapes seemed to move as the lamp sputtered and the flame wavered.

'Who made these pictures?' Willow gasped.

'Your father,' Rainbow told him.

'But how?'

The woman sat on the floor of the cave beside some small stone pots. 'I would grind up coloured rock in these. Then I added water and your father put the colour on the wall... sometimes he dipped moss in the colours, sometimes he filled his mouth with the colour and blew it through a hollow bone.'

'They're wonderful,' Willow said. 'Why have you brought me here?'

Rainbow nodded slowly. 'This must be your new home. You are safe from Bull down here. I will bring you food and water each day and new fat for your lamp.'

'And will you mix the colours for me?'
the boy asked.

The woman laughed softly. 'You want

to make pictures the way your father did?' she asked.

'I want to try,' he said.

'Good. The tribe needs someone,' she told him.

'Do they?'

'Oh yes,' she went on. 'The pictures tell the story of our lives. Look, there are hunters chasing horses,' she said pointing to a group of black figures with spears. 'The great spirits see them. It pleases them. They give us luck.'

Willow ran his finger around the dry paint in the bowl and frowned. 'We have had no luck. Today we did catch a bison... but our leader Flint died.'

Rainbow nodded her head wisely. 'Yes, because no one has been making new pictures since your father died. You must try, son.'

Willow breathed in deeply. 'I have never

been a powerful hunter,' he said. 'But this feels good.'

'It's what you were born to do, my son. Your father would have taught you once you were old enough, just as his father taught him. But he died too soon. You must teach yourself. You can do it. The great spirit will guide you.'

Willow nodded. 'The great spirit will guide me. I can do it.'

'Rest tonight. Tomorrow you start. I will

bring you food and mix your paint at sunrise.'

And so Willow began his new life in the great cavern.

7

Deer

As winter grew colder, Willow was warm enough in his cave. It was warmer than the huts of the village when the wind blew cruelly from the north.

Each day Rainbow brought him food and news. Each day he painted more and drew scenes that he remembered. His mother raised a lamp and looked up

at the painting he was finishing. 'That man is falling,' she said.

'Yes, it is Flint when he was charged by the bison. He was a good leader. I want to remember him.'

Rainbow nodded, silent.

A week later she hurried in with fresh meat, still warm from the roasting fire. 'It is working, Willow. Your pictures are pleasing the spirits. They have sent a herd of horse and deer into the valley. They sheltered from a rain storm. But the rain made the earth slide down the hillside and blocked the end of the valley.'

Willow nodded, eager. 'So, if we build a fence at this end, the horses and deer will be trapped. We won't have to go over the mountains to hunt. We can take them one at a time to get us through the winter.'

His mother nodded, 'That was Owl's idea. The tribe will be well fed this winter.'

Suddenly a deeper voice rang through the cave. 'So this is where you've been hiding little Willow, is it?'

Rainbow swung round and the lamp shone into the small eyes of Bull. He stepped down the slope to the floor of the cave.

'Sorry, Willow,' the woman said quickly to her son. 'I was so excited I forgot to look to see if I was followed.'

'I said I would kill you,' Bull snarled.

Rainbow rose to her feet and blocked the young chief's path. 'This is the cavern of the spirits. Willow is in their care. If you hurt him, you will anger the spirits. And when the spirits grow angry the whole tribe will suffer. Winds will blow down our huts. Snow will block us into the valley till we freeze and starve. And the tribe will blame you, Bull. The ones who live through the winter will say it was all Bull's fault.'

The hunter looked unsure. His voice turned to a whine. 'I didn't say I would harm poor Willow. I mean, I did say that. But I heard what you said about his paintings bringing us luck.' He looked around the cave and wondered at the paintings. He saw the image of the falling man. 'Poor old Flint.'

'He will be remembered,' Willow said.

Bull whispered. 'Will I? When the

spirits take me twenty winters from now – will the tribe remember me?'

Willow smiled. 'They will if I draw you hunting deer. If I draw you running fast as a horse with your spear in your mighty arm.'

'My mighty arm,' Bull sighed and his eyes shone orange-yellow in the light of the flame. 'Oh, Willow, we grew up together. You were always my dearest friend. I have missed you since you fled from the village. Will you come back with me now?'

Willow nodded his head. 'I love this work but I do feel lonely. It would be good to see our people again.'

Bull nodded, eager. 'I shall hunt and you shall paint. Together we shall rule the tribe.'

'Together?' Rainbow asked.

'Yes. Willow shall be the chief when I am away hunting. Will you do that, Willow?'

Willow looked at his mother and there was laughter in her eyes. 'I could do that,' he said.

Bull's round face shone, happy. 'And when will you paint my picture on the walls of the cave of the spirits?'

'Tomorrow, Bull, tomorrow,' the painter promised.

Bull marched up the ramp into the cold evening air. Willow looked at his mother, who was staring into the gloom as if she could see the great spirit there. 'Be happy, mother.'

She sighed. 'I can be happy for you, Willow. I can be happy for me. But I am worried for the men and women of this world. How will they ever last through time?'

'Why shouldn't they?' the boy asked.

Rainbow looked at the back of the vanishing Bull. 'Because the people with power are all such fools.'

Willow shook his head. 'Let's go home, mother. Let's go home.'

The True Story

In 1940, during World War II, four teenage boys were hunting in woods in Lascaux, France. Suddenly, their dog vanished into a hole at the foot of a cliff face. They climbed down and rescued the dog.

The hole was the entrance to a cave. They had discovered one of the greatest cave-art displays of all time: the Lascaux caves. The boys kept their secret for a week and then told their teacher. Experts went into the caves and said the paintings were 17,000 years old. Visitors flocked in. They carried their germs with them, and these formed a green mould all over the ancient artwork. The caves were closed and sealed.

The Lascaux caves were painted in the New Stone Age. The deeper parts of the cave were lit by lamps that burned animal fat, but the New Stone Age people didn't live in the caves and we don't know why they painted the animals and humans. It may have been a message to their gods, asking for good luck with the hunt.

The main colours used were reds, yellows, and blacks. The painters used coloured rocks that they crushed and painted onto the walls of the underground passages. Some were drawn with fingers dipped in the paint, and some with sticks charred in the fire (charcoal). The Stone Age artists also made brushes of hair or moss. Sometimes they blew their paint through a hollow bone.

The caves contain 2,000 paintings of animals, humans and symbols. The pictures show a lot of horses, cows, bison, deer and creatures like cats. One of them shows a hunter being killed by a bison: a falling man.

This story tells how that man may have died, and how the first pictures were made. It is just a story, but the caves and the wonderful paintings are real.

YOU TRY...

1. PAINT

You can find pictures of the Lascaux Caves in books or on the internet. They look simple – but try to make copies in the same way the Lascaux artists did, and you will find they were very clever!

Take a large sheet of paper or card. Use just three colours: red, yellow and black. Use a straw to spray paint, a cloth to dab it on, or your fingers to smear the paint.

Could you be a cave painter?

2. REPORT

Imagine you were one of the French boys who found the Lascaux Caves in 1940. You have just reported it to your schoolmaster, and he asks you to write down exactly what happened before you forget. Write your report in 200 words or less.

3. PLAN

Draw a map of an area of countryside. It has hills and a valley with cliffs on either side, a stream and a forest, a village (where you and your tribe live) and footpaths that have been worn out of the grassland by animals. On the plan, there are a few horses in the valley.

Stone-Age people would creep up on the animals; then they'd drive them over the cliffs. To do this, they'd have to work as a team. When you have drawn your plan, share it with a friend or two. Plan how you could work together to drive the animals over the cliff so you can eat them!

Here's the catch: you can only use five words, no more! (Maybe 'you', 'me', 'cattle', 'run', and 'cliffs' – or a different five of your own.) Now share your plan with your hunting friends. If you use more than five words, you lose!

Terry Deary's Stone Age Tales

ISBN: 978 1 4729 5026 0

ISBN: 978 1 4729 5031 4

ISBN: 978 1 4729 5035 2

ISBN: 978 1 4729 5040 6

Look out for more exciting
stories set in the Stone Age!